This book belongs to

....

Written by Tim Bugbird.
Illustrated by Lara Ede.
Designed by Gabrielle Mercer.

Copyright © 2012

make believe ideas ltd

The Wilderness, Berkhamsted, Hertfordshire, HP4 2AZ, UK.
565 Royal Parkway, Nashville, TN 37214, USA.

www.makebelieveideas.com

Lola the Lollipop Fairy

Tim Bugbird · Lara Ede

make believe ideas

Once upon a time
in a circus big top,
lived a fairy family,
the sisters Lollipop!

Every day at **six o'clock**,
come rain or shine or snow,
fairies came from *far* and *wide*
to see their famous show!

Show

6pm

Lola was the one in charge

and **Linda** lifted weights.

Lulu juggled lollipops
and sometimes spinning plates!

Their act had been the same for years
and their tent was worn and old,
but every night they did their best
and all the seats were sold.

'Til one morning Lola woke;
she **yawned** and rubbed her eye:
She looked outside and had a **shock**
what a bad surprise!

Next door, where the grass had been,
the plants and trees and flowers,
there stood a brand-new theme park
with rides and slides and towers!

cat bed

The park became
the **place to go**,
where fairies met to play,
and **no one**
came to Lola's show.
She sighed, as if to say,
"The rides are so exciting,
we just cannot **compete**."
Lulu said, "Let's face it, friends,
I think we might be **beat**!"

"So we'll just make our show better!"
Lola boldly cried.
"We'll do our best, so if we fail,
at least we'll know we tried!"

"Let's think of something **super big**,
a **spectacular** creation,
a show to make the fairies talk —
we'll be the new **sensation!**"

In a flash it came to Lola –
a plan to make them swoon.
Lola the Fairy Cannonball
would fly up to the moon!

So the fairies built a **cannon**
that was just the perfect size
to fire fearless Lola
from the circus to the skies!
They **banged** and **bashed**,
and **clanged** and **clashed**
until the job was done.
The work was **hard**,
the hours were **long**,
but they'd never had *such fun*!

The day for launching Lola
came around really fast.
Linda hollered, "Three, two, one!"
and, with a deafening BLAST,

Lola shot up into space as the fairies waved and cheered.

And Lola thought, "What a lovely place, I'm glad I volunteered!"

And when Lola finally landed, she cried:
"Oh my goodness, golly!
I thought the moon was made of cheese,
but it's a great big orange lolly!"

It certainly was the sweetest place
Lola had **ever seen**,
with **lollipops** of every kind
and mountains of whipped **cream!**

The **air** was
sweet as strawberries
and the **sky** was
pink and **clear**.
Lola flew back down to earth —
she'd had a **new idea**.

Her cannon show had been a blast,

but this plan was the ace.

They'd make their fairy fortunes

firing fairies into space!

And so the sisters got to work, they never seemed to stop.
Soon the moon trips made enough to buy a

new BIG TOP!

With a brand-new sparkly cannon, glitter, and lights aglow,
very soon the stage was set for their amazing circus show!

It was thrilling and exciting, a full house every night.
The fairies saved the circus thanks to Lola's daring flight!

So Lola, Linda, and Lulu made the perfect team.

By working hard, and not giving up, they lived their fairy dream!